How the True Facts Started in Simpsonville and Other Tales of the West

How the True Facts Started in Simpsonville and Other Tales of the West

William D. Hayes

Atheneum   1972   New York

Contents

*How the True Facts Started in
Simpsonville*   *1*

*How Bart Winslow Single Handed
Wiped Out the Jimson Gang,
Which Was Known as the Scourge
of the West*   *10*

*How the Sneaky Water-Stealer Set the
Cattlemen and the Sheepmen Against
Each Other*   *24*

*How the Ranchers of Windy Canyon
Built the Biggest Fence the West
Has Ever Seen*   *37*

*How Matt Carney Retired and Raised
Chickens*   *54*

*How Ailments Were Put in Their
Proper Place*   *70*

*How the Sheriff's Posse and the Hold-up
Men Sat Down to Dinner Together*   *81*

How the True Facts Started in Simpsonville and Other Tales of the West

How the True Facts Started in Simpsonville

You're a liar!"

Big Jim Beeler said the words slow and deliberate, and he looked the stranger straight in the eye.

The other men in Aunt Marcy's Home-Style Café backed away.

Beeler and the stranger stood there facing each other steady and calm. The place was quiet as moonlight.

The stranger smiled. "Gentlemen," he said, "I have the highest respect for Simpsonville.

Your love for honesty and veracity is known all over the West. But I swear I took a drink from the Hassayampa River."

"Well," said Lafe Brimhall, "he's a nice polite liar, anyway."

Some of the men laughed, and it eased the situation a little.

"And he understands about our honesty and veracity," said Bart Winslow.

"Stranger," Beeler said, "did you ever hear the saying that if a man drinks from the Hassayampa he'll never again tell the truth?"

"Sure," the stranger said. "Everybody's heard that. But it's just a saying."

"No," Beeler said. "It's the truth. And that's because there isn't any water in the Hassayampa. Never has been. Not so far as anybody recollects, that is."

"But I saw it," the stranger said. "I drank some, and I was still thirsty. So I drank some more. I drank and I drank, and I . . ."

"And I know you didn't," Beeler cut in. "And if a man claims he drank from a river that hasn't got any water in it—well, anybody can see that he's such an all-fired liar he'll never again tell the truth. And that's how that saying got started about drinking from the Hassayampa."

"It pains me for you to doubt my word," the stranger said. "If you gentlemen will just come along with me, I will show you the very place where I drank from the Hassayampa."

"Boys," said Bart Winslow, "this stranger seems like a nice fellow. And in spite of the fact that he is a bare-faced liar, I want to find out what this is all about. I think we ought to accept his invitation and go down to the river."

So they followed the stranger out of the café. The screen door slammed seventeen times. Aunt Marcy winced as she counted them off. Beeler grumbled a little, but he went along, too.

The board sidewalk rumbled and creaked as the men headed down Main Street. Past the big front window of the *Tri-Weekly Bugle and Gazette*—"All the News That's Fit to Print in the West"—they went, past Judge Harper's fine house with the cast iron fence, and on out past the livery stable.

Clouds of dust rolled up around them. The stranger coughed. "Driest place I ever saw," he said. "Why, a while ago I saw a whirlwind dust-devil whirling around and drilling itself right into the ground. Drilling for water, it was."

Will Kingman glanced at Bart Winslow. Bart was Will's foreman out at the B-Bar-X ranch. They shook their heads in a pitying way. "Poor fellow," Will whispered. "He wouldn't know the truth if he met it in the middle of the street."

They followed the stranger along by the bare rocks and the dusty tamarisk trees. There wasn't a sound except the *squnch-squnch* of boots in the dry river bed.

After a while the stranger stopped and pointed. "There," he said. "Right there is where I drank."

At this, the men all folded up and laughed fit to bust.

"Stranger," Beeler said when he could catch his breath, "don't you know a mirage when you see one?"

4

"Mirage?" said the stranger. "What's a mirage?"

"A mirage, friend," said Bart Winslow, "is something that looks like water but isn't. It's a kind of optical illusion. We've got lots of them here in the West."

Bart stooped down and scooped up some of the mirage in his hands. "You see, friend," he said, "you could drink this stuff all day and it wouldn't quench your thirst—for the simple reason that there isn't any water in it. It just looks like water. It's nothing but an optical illusion. Let's show him, boys."

So they all scooped up some of the optical illusion, and they all drank from that mirage in the Hassayampa.

Now as soon as the stranger saw his mistake, he was all apologies. "I sure am sorry I led you gentlemen on a wild goose chase," he said. "I'm a ring-tailed horned toad if I ever saw anything like this before."

"Don't let it bother you, friend," Bart Winslow said in a kindly manner. "You are not a ring-tailed horned toad. You simply made a mistake that any stranger could have made. And we want you to know that you are welcome in Simpsonville, just as long as you stick strictly to the true facts. Right, Beeler?"

"Right," Beeler said. "Just don't forget it, stranger." Then Beeler scratched his head, thoughtful like. "Speaking of true facts," he said, "I just remembered something I clean forgot to mention before. Something this stranger said a while ago—that's what reminded me of it."

"You mean that whirlwind dust-devil?" Will Kingman said.

"Exactly," Beeler said. "I'm beginning to recollect something about that time the dust-devils were so bad. There must have been millions of them that year. Maybe more. And some of them were so thick and so tall they clean shut out the light of day."

"They sure did," Lafe Brimhall said. "And speaking of shutting out the light of day, do you recall the time all those wild geese flew over?"

"How could we forget it?" Will Kingman

said. "The sky was black with them. Fact is, the days were as dark as the nights. The fireflies flew around all lighted up in the daytime."

"That's right," Bart Winslow said, "there were so many of those geese flying south for the winter, they didn't all get past before they had to turn around and come back up north for the summer."

The stranger listened with deep interest to all these true facts.

Well, then the others began to remember things that happened a while back, too. And by the time they reached the edge of town, they were all remembering a whole lot of things they had forgotten to mention before.

When they came blustering along Main Street, spouting off a lot of facts that had never been heard around Simpsonville before, folks were mighty shocked.

Mayor Hawkins glared at the whole bunch of them. "Beeler," he called out, "sounds to me like you fools have been drinking from the Hassayampa."

8

Well, that's how it started, and that's where it started.

Pretty soon, people in other parts of the West were repeating the true facts that were told to them by Beeler and the others in Simpsonville. That's because a lot of people everywhere knew about the honesty and veracity of Simpsonville, and they knew that if the folks in Simpsonville said something was true, well, it must be true.

Then it wasn't long before the West was famous all over the world for its particular brand of true facts.

How Bart Winslow Single Handed Wiped Out the Jimson Gang, Which Was Known as the Scourge of the West

They went in singin', and they came out singin'.

That's the way it was with the Jimson gang.

All up and down the western lands they roamed, thieving, robbing and shooting—and singing about it all the time. Always singing about it.

Every once in a while the Jimson gang got around to playing the towns along the Hassa-yampa River, with more than ordinary atten-tion to Simpsonville. Folks always said their thieving and robbing and shooting wasn't near as bad as their singing.

There was one Jimson called Shorty. And there was Curly and Skinny. Some folks said there were six of them all together. And others said there were only five—they just sounded like six. They would tear into Simpsonville and out again so fast nobody could tell for sure how many of them there were.

Like the time they shot their way into the Wells Fargo office on Main Street. They went in plunking on their guitars and singing a twangy song.

"Oh we got to rob, and that's a fact,
Oh why do we do such a no-good,
infernal, low-down act?"

And while they gathered up the Wells Fargo gold shipment, they sang about how they were born under the wrong kind of a star and how they were just no account and were bound to lose in the long run no matter how hard they tried to be good.

As they were leaving with the gold, they fired a few shots at the windows and other glassware just to be ornery. Then they rode off singing.

Well, Sheriff Hardesty didn't have any trouble tracking them down. All he had to do was follow that sorrowful sad twanging. And when he had them cornered in Windy Canyon they sang,

"Oh we're tracked down and caught and
we ain't got no hope,
And we'll prob'ly swing at the end of
a rope."

So the sheriff locked the Jimson gang in jail, and everybody was glad about it. But pretty soon there came that sorrowful sad singing and twanging. Folks stopped up their ears, but that didn't help. The more they tried not to listen, the more the song grated on their backbones. Loud and clear it floated out of the jail and all through Simpsonville:

> *"Oh we got them jailhouse blues,*
> *Blue as blue can be,*
> *And we ain't no good at all—*
> *fer as we can see."*

Well, the jailer sat there like the singing didn't make any difference to him at all. He rustled through a newspaper and peered at it like he was concentrating something fierce on all the fascinating news items in it, and like he didn't even know the Jimson gang was there, and like he wasn't listening to that twanging at all.

But he was listening, all right. And finally the day came when he knew he couldn't stand that singing any longer. He grabbed the keys and opened that cell door fast.

"Get out o' here, you howlin' coyotes!" he yelled. And he landed a kick square on Shorty's hind parts to help him through the door.

The gang rode off wailing and twanging.

Well, the Simpsonville jailer wasn't the only jailer that couldn't stand to listen to that kind of singing. And pretty soon there wasn't a jail in the West that could hold the Jimson gang for long. That's the way it was with the Jimson gang. They went in singin', and they came out singin'. They were known as the scourge of the West.

One day Bart Winslow and a bunch of the men from the ranches in Windy Canyon were riding toward Simpsonville. Up ahead Bart saw the Jimson gang holding up the Tombstone stage. Well, that is, he heard them before he actually saw them. And Bart didn't have to listen twice to know who it was and what they were up to.

"Quick, men!" Bart said. "Let's catch those varmints and put them where they belong, once and for all."

"Wait," said Slim Pickens. "What's the use of putting them in jail? There isn't a sheriff this side of anywhere that'll keep those coyotes locked up once they start that howling and moaning."

"Then we'll build a special jail," Bart said. "Just for the Jimson gang. Out where nobody has to listen to them. But first we've got to catch them. Are you with me, boys?"

A mighty cheer went up, and they took off fast.

But by the time they got to the stagecoach the Jimson gang was gone.

"They got every last cent of the Vulture Mine payroll," the driver told Bart.

Bart dismounted and put his ear to the ground. "Good way to tell which way they went," he said. "Learned this trick from an old Indian scout."

"They went that way," the driver said, pointing.

"Any fool knows that," said Old Dan Frazzle. "You can hear them howlin' plain as day."

So Bart and the men followed the mournful sounds. Pretty soon they came to a lonely shack by the Hassayampa River. And out of that shack came a song:

"Oh we got away,
But we done wrong like we always done
—and we got to pay."

The wailing and whining song had a lot of verses, and the Jimsons didn't skip a single one. Bart set his jaw firm. "Remember, men," he said, "time is on our side. They can't eat that payroll money. And sooner or later they've got to come out of there for grub and drinking water."

So the men took up positions around the shack and settled down to wait it out. And all the time that rasping and twanging never let up for a second.

Pretty soon the coyotes started howling out there on the desert in the middle of the day, right in tune with the twanging. And the owls flew out of the cottonwoods and moved down river to a quieter place where owls could sleep in the daytime the way owls ought to do.

The men squared their shoulders and tried to brush the singing away like it was something crawling around on them.

Bart got sadder and sadder listening to the Jimson gang singing about how there wasn't any hope for them, and how they weren't ever loved by anybody except maybe their mother, and how she didn't work any too hard at it either as a matter of fact.

Bart watched the men as they waited. Their faces grew stony and grim. "I don't see how they can stand to listen to that sad stuff much longer," Bart said to himself. "For that matter, I don't see how I can stand it, either."

The Jimson gang was on the twenty-eighth verse of "I Got Them Down-in-the-Mouth, Down-at-the-Heels, Nobody-Never-Loved-Me-Nohow, Never-Can-Win, Born-to-Lose Blues" when all of a sudden Slim Pickens jumped up. "I can't stand it!" Slim yelled. "I can't stand to listen to any more of that. Why, I'd rather they'd

Track me down and shoot me dead,
The cold, cold ground to rest my—

Now they've got me doing it," he said. "I'm getting out of here fast." And Slim jumped on his horse and galloped off for Simpsonville.

A minute later it was Lafe Brimhall. And then Brod Reed rode off through the cactus,

blubbering right out loud.

After a while Bart was left standing there all by himself with nothing to keep him company but the sandy bed of the Hassayampa and the cottonwoods and cactus and tamarisks, and all those mournful sounds coming out of that shack.

The shadows of the cottonwoods and tamarisks stretched themselves long over the Hassayampa. Finally Bart said to himself, "I can't take any more of this. And besides, what can one man do against five or six, anyhow? I guess I'll have to give up just like . . ."

Bart stopped.

He had an idea.

It might work.

He cupped his hands to his mouth. He yelled toward the shack, "Hey, you in there! Hey, you Jimsons! Listen to me. You know what I think? I think Shorty sings louder and sadder than all the rest of you put together. Lots louder and lots sadder."

Bart waited. After a few seconds the singing stopped, and everything was quiet as a shadow. It was so quiet around there the birds came out of the trees and looked around to see what was wrong.

Suddenly a lot of yelling came out of that shack. Then one voice boomed out louder than the others. "You heard the man. Ain't I always said I sing the loudest and saddest?"

Bart smiled.

"You don't, neither," another voice yelled.

"I do, so."

"No, you don't."

"Yes, I do."

There was a shot.

Bart ducked behind a cactus.

Then a couple of more shots. Then a whole lot more. Then there was one last shot. Then quiet.

Bart waited. He thought he heard a horse gallop away, but he couldn't be sure. He stepped out from behind the cactus. He walked slow toward the shack, his hands on his holsters.

Slow and cautious he walked up to the door. He listened. There wasn't any sound except the heavy silence.

Bart drew both guns.

He kicked the door in.

He waited.

Nothing but silence.

He stepped inside.

The Jimson gang lay there all still and quiet, their guitars splintered with bullet holes. Dust and smoke settled down over the peaceful scene. Bart noticed there were only five lying there.

Well, pretty soon some of the men in town came riding out to see what all the shooting was about. And when they got a look inside that shack they gave a whoop that was heard clear over in Pinal County.

Months later, reports reached Simpsonville that back East somebody was going around singing a lot of sorrowful sad songs—songs about being born to lose and how there wasn't any use trying at all and a lot of sad things like that. Reports came in from Kansas City and Nashville and Boston and a lot of famous places.

One day a traveling man in Aunt Marcy's café said the people back East actually seemed to *like* that kind of singing.

Bart bristled. "Now, look here!" he said. "This is my native land and I love it. And I don't cotton to anybody saying things like that about it."

The traveling man took one look around at the stony faces staring at him and he gulped down his steak and eggs and he got out of there fast.

Simpsonville folks felt mighty sorry for the Easterners.

But they were real glad to have things quiet and peaceful again at home. And they gave Bart all the credit.

Bart kept insisting that he wasn't any hero. He tried to tell them exactly what happened out there at that shack. But nobody listened.

Before long it was unanimous. And after that everybody said that Bart Winslow single handed wiped out the Jimson gang, which was known as the scourge of the West.

How the Sneaky Water-Stealer Set the Cattlemen and the Sheepmen Against Each Other

The Hassayampa wasn't the only river in the West that didn't have any water in it. Not by a long shot. And there came a time when the wells and water holes were going dry, too.

Folks in Simpsonville more or less expected Bart Winslow to come up with a way to solve the problem. Now, Bart didn't have any more idea what to do about the water shortage than the next fellow. But everybody knew Bart was the man who single handed wiped out the Jimson gang, which was known as the scourge of

24

the West. So, naturally, folks considered Bart an expert on everything, including the water problem.

The bone-dry water shortage began to cause a lot of mighty hard feelings. The cattlemen said the sheepmen were stealing all the water. And the sheepmen said the cattlemen were stealing it all. Things got tense and more tense until nerves were strung tight as a fiddle string.

Now, the biggest cattleman in the territory was Matt Carney.

One day Carney rode into town shouting a lot of insulting things about sheepmen. Folks could hear him yelling clear from the Wells Fargo office at one end of town to the livery stable at the other. Carney stood right in the middle of Main Street, ankle-deep in dust, and yelled, "All sheepmen are low-down thieving water-stealers. And none of them better ever cross my path. And that goes especially for Brod Reed."

Carney emphasized the point by patting his gun holster.

Now, everybody knew that Brod Reed was

the biggest sheepman in the territory.

Some of the boys rode out to Reed's place and just happened to mention what Carney had said.

Not long after that, Reed stood in the same spot on Main Street where Carney had stood. "All cattlemen are yellow-bellied sniveling water-stealers," Reed yelled. "I'd go hunt them all down right now—except that I just plain can't tell them from the cattle. And that goes especially for Matt Carney."

Some of the boys rode out to Carney's spread and advised him of what Reed had said.

Before long, the social arrangements were made, and Carney and Reed agreed to shoot it out on Main Street the following day at noon.

"Tomorrow noon!" Bart Winslow said when he heard about it out at the B-Bar-X. "That doesn't give me much time. But if somebody doesn't do something to stop that gun duel, we could have the biggest range war the West has ever seen."

"Look, Bart," Will Kingman said, "Carney and Reed are shooting mad. Nobody can stop that gun duel now. Not even you."

"I can try," Bart said. "There's something mighty peculiar about all that water disappearing. Maybe it isn't the cattlemen or the sheepmen either one that's to blame."

So, while folks in town prepared for the social event that was to take place the next day at noon, Bart took off from the ranch. He rode out past Razorback Ridge. He studied the mountains and the sky, and he studied the rain clouds over Old Four Peaks.

All that night Bart rode over the hills watching those rain clouds.

Along about sunup the sky over Old Four Peaks split itself wide open with thunder and lightning. The clouds poured down their rain.

A few drops fell around Bart. But most of that rain funneled itself down toward just one place. Bart picked out a landmark that was right in the middle of where that rain was funneling. The landmark was a tall tamarisk tree.

Bart left his horse at ground-hitch and made his way to the tamarisk. There wasn't a drop

of water in sight. He stomped his feet. Dust curled up from the dry hot ground.

"Something must have soaked that rain right out of the air," Bart said to himself.

He looked at the rocks and the ground, and he looked up and down that tamarisk. But there wasn't a sign of where all that rain had gone.

The early morning sun bore down hot. Bart mopped the sweat from his face with a bandana. He went around and sat down on the shady side of the tree. That is, it *should* have been the shady side. As Bart took a sip of water from his canteen he realized something.

There wasn't any shade.

Where the shade ought to be, there wasn't anything but sunshine.

Bart set his canteen down. He stared up at the branches. "Amazing!" he said to himself.

"All that rain disappearing! A tree without any shade! I wonder if . . ."

A rustling sound made Bart freeze. He didn't move, except to look in the direction of the rustling sound.

And what to his amazement did he see but a root of that big tamarisk tree poking up right out of the ground and waving from side to side.

The root waved around in the air a few seconds. Then it leveled out and stretched along close to the ground. It came snaking right toward Bart's canteen.

When it reached the canteen, the root raised up and hovered there. It moved from side to side. Then it twisted itself right around the lid.

Bart could hardly believe his eyes.

That root unscrewed the lid and set it carefully on the ground. The root poked itself down inside and slurped every drop of water out of that canteen. Then it picked up the lid and screwed it back on.

The root slithered away, slow and sneaky, like it knew it was being watched.

When it was back where it came from, it wiggled around and settled itself down into the ground. And there it stayed, all still and innocent like.

Bart scooched around to find some shade. Then he remembered. There wasn't any shade.

"Why, a tree like that," he said out loud, "a tree that drinks the rain before it gets to the ground, and uses up all its own shade, and steals the water right out of a man's canteen—a tree like that could almost . . ."

Bart jumped up. He looked at his railroad dollar watch that he got from a mail order house in Kansas City.

There wasn't any time to lose.

Back in Simpsonville the folks were gathering along Main Street for the big social event—the shoot-out between Matt Carney and Brod Reed. The loose board in front of the Elite Hotel had kept up a steady clatter since sunup. There were even some folks who came all the way from Pinal County.

Everybody was all dyked out in his picnic clothes, and there was a brass band, such as Simpsonville had to offer. All in all it was turning into a right gala occasion.

Along toward noon the festivities quieted down. The loose board was still. The ring of the blacksmith's hammer stopped. The horses stopped whinnying. A kind of hushed silence settled over Simpsonville.

Matt Carney stood at one end of Main Street at the Wells Fargo office.

Brod Reed stood at the other end of the street at the livery stable.

The big bank clock struck noon.

Carney and Reed started walking toward each other.

The only sound was the jangle of spurs as each step closed the distance between them.

They walked in a slow measured rhythm, like counting the seconds till one or the other would die.

The place was so quiet you could almost hear a shadow on the wall.

"Stop!" somebody yelled.

Carney and Reed crouched.

"Stop!"

It was Bart Winslow.

Bart ran into the street. He jumped between Carney and Reed.

"Bart!" Carney yelled. "You trying to get your head shot off?"

"Beat it, Bart!" Reed yelled. "This is a private matter."

"Listen, everybody!" Bart shouted. "The water! I found out what's happening to all the water. And it isn't the cattlemen or the sheepmen, either, that's stealing it."

Well, at first folks were mighty sore at Bart for breaking up their social event. They grumbled as they came down off the sidewalk into the street. But they stopped grumbling when Bart told them about the rain funneling down toward that big tamarisk, and how it used up all its own shade, and how that root stole the water right out of his canteen.

There probably wasn't another man in the territory who could have got away with breaking up that social event. But everybody knew that Bart was the man who single handed wiped out the Jimson gang, which was known as the scourge of the West.

Bart took Carney and Reed and Mayor Hawkins and Judge Harper and a lot of other folks out for a close look at the wells and water holes. The roots of that one tamarisk had reached out for miles. Every one of those dry wells and water holes had a tamarisk root growing in it.

Finally Bart said to Carney and Reed, "Boys, I think it's time for you two to shake hands."

Carney and Reed looked down at the ground and scrubbed their toes in the dust. They grinned and shook hands.

It wasn't any easy job to get rid of that big tamarisk tree that was stealing the rain and most of the water for miles around. But Bart and a bunch of the men finally sawed clean through the trunk. That tree was so tall and fell so far and hit so hard it split the ground wide open and sprung out some new springs of water that nobody knew about up to that time.

It wasn't long before some false rumors got started about that big tamarisk.

One rumor was that the entire Petrified Forest was caused by just the twigs off of that one tree. Another rumor was that when the men dug out the stump it left a hole so big it became the Grand Canyon. Now, it's just this kind of irresponsible reporting that makes people distrustful of things they hear in the West.

Well, Carney and Reed got to be right good friends. In fact, a lot of cattlemen and sheepmen got to be good friends.

But there are still some people who think the cattlemen got most of the water in the early days. And there are others who think the sheepmen weren't entirely blameless, either, for that matter.

They think this in spite of the fact that you can still see offspring of that big tamarisk tree growing in the dry river and creek beds all over the West.

How the Ranchers
of Windy Canyon
Built the Biggest Fence
the West Has Ever Seen

It wasn't always just natural enemies like sheepmen and cattlemen that had their troubles.

Will Kingman and Mario Sanchez, for instance. They were both cattlemen. And they were good friends—at first.

Their two ranch houses stood just outside of Simpsonville in Windy Canyon, in the dry and sandy land between the Jagged Mountains. It was called Windy Canyon because the wind sometimes blew up the canyon toward the east, and sometimes blew down the canyon toward the west.

When the wind and sand blew right hard up the canyon toward the east, the chickens, ducks, geese and cats of the B-Bar-X ranch blew over onto the B-Bar-Bar ranch. And when the wind blew right hard down the canyon toward the west, the chickens, ducks, geese and cats from the B-Bar-Bar blew over onto the B-Bar-X.

One morning the wind was blowing down the canyon toward the west. Slick Smith the peddler stopped his buggy on a road on one of the Jagged Mountains. The peddler looked down on the two ranches. Chickens, ducks, geese and cats from the B-Bar-Bar were flying over onto the B-Bar-X.

The peddler watched this for a while and scratched his head. "Why do you suppose those animals are flying through the air?" he said to his horse, but the horse did not answer.

"We will go down and see about this," said the peddler, and with a flick of the reins they were off down the hill toward the ranch houses.

The buggy was painted with signs and curli-cue dingbats. *Slick Smith,* it said. *Leather Boots, Candy, Can Openers, Frying Pans* and *FENCES.*

"Fences," said the peddler as he pulled up near the barn of the B-Bar-X. "That's what people need here in the West. Fences are a very civilizing influence."

Rancher Will Kingman was helping his neighbor Mario Sanchez round up the animals. They lassoed a long-whiskered billy goat and herded a flock of wildly fluttering hens toward the B-Bar-Bar.

"Fences?" asked Will Kingman.

"Fences?" asked Mario Sanchez.

"Fences," said Slick Smith the peddler.

"What have you got in that sample case," asked Kingman, leaning over to see better, "and why do we need fences? Friendship is all the fence we need."

"Right," Sanchez agreed. "Friendship and understanding are better than all the fences in the world. Why should we need fences?"

"To protect your property," Slick Smith

said, "and to keep your animals at home. And besides," he added, "it's more civilized." He was busy polishing a new patented potato peeler. "You will need a good high fence to protect your land," said the peddler. "I happen to have a sample right here." He picked up a shiny piece of barbed wire and held it high.

"Well, now," said Kingman. "I don't believe in fences, but I guess I could use a couple of hundred feet of the wire. We could run it right between the barns there. Might help keep our animals at home when the breeze comes up." He and Mr. Sanchez chuckled.

The peddler began to write in a thick order book. "By the way," he said, "do I see different brands on the cattle over there at that water hole?"

"That's right," Kingman said. "Some of those critters have Mr. Sanchez' brand, and some of them have mine. You see, the water hole is practically on the property line."

"Then which ever one of you gentlemen owns that water hole," said the peddler, "if you would put a good barbed wire fence right up to the bluff over there, it would really protect that water."

"I never thought of that," Sanchez said. "A good strong fence might keep Mr. Kingman's cattle from tracking up the best water hole in the West. It's on my property."

"Now, just a thunderin' minute here!" Kingman said. "Talk about a water hole! What about Blue Canyon? Those critters of yours think they own Blue Canyon."

"Fine grazing land like Blue Canyon ought to be protected with a good fence," the peddler said.

Sanchez snorted. "Blue Canyon! Weed Gulch, I call it!"

"Is that so?" Kingman said. His face turned a kind of a sunset purple. "It's nine miles to Blue Canyon, and I want every foot of it fenced —clear from here to there. You got that down, Mr. Peddler?"

"I've got it," Slick Smith said, writing fast. "By the way, which one of you gentlemen owns Razorback Ridge?"

"Half of it's mine," Sanchez said. "No use fencing that. It's nothing but forty miles of useless rock."

"Useless rock?" Kingman shouted, throwing his hands in the air. "It hasn't been two years since I found some of your boys prospecting for gold on my side of that ridge. The fence goes through. All the way. Clear to the Tonto Rim!"

"Hm-m-m," the peddler said, writing very fast, "and how about the property line south of here?"

"Fence it!" both men shouted. "Fence it clear to the border!"

"This is the smartest thing you ranchers ever did," the peddler said when he had finished writing the long order. "You'll get a notice from the railroad when your fence arrives. Be sure to come haul it away as soon as you can. Don't want all those freight cars tied up too long."

Well, when that train load of barbed wire showed up, all hands on both ranches were called in from the range. Every man went to work putting up that fence.

Bart Winslow, the B-Bar-X foreman, started his men south toward the border. Mario Sanchez' men moved north from the B-Bar-Bar. On through the pass to Blue Canyon they built the fence, a post every five paces. Slim Pickens, the B-Bar-Bar foreman, paced off the distance between post holes. His legs were longer than anybody's. He could take big steps, and this meant fewer holes to dig.

The men worked fast and hard.

On they went, digging, shoveling, hammering. Over the dry bed of the Hassayampa, past Blue Canyon and on across Razorback Ridge they went, and beyond, until after a while the fence stretched away as far as an eagle could see.

When the work was done, the two ranchers

were so proud they forgot they were mad at each other. They looked at the shiny wire stretching away to the north and to the south.

"This is the biggest fence the West has ever seen or ever will see," said Sanchez. "Slick Smith was right. This is the civilized way to do things."

"It is that," said Kingman. And they reached through the fence and shook hands.

Visitors came from far away to see that fence. It was written up in the Simpsonville *Gazette* and other famous newspapers, until it was known everywhere as the biggest fence in the West.

All went well for awhile. The work on the two ranches went along the way work ought to go. There were the horses to feed, the cattle to round up. There were the cows to milk, the buildings to paint, the bunkhouses to keep clean. There were barn dances to go to, and there were church picnics and box socials.

But then things began to change.

Both ranchers noticed it at about the same

time. They saw that the ranch hands were not bustling around the way they did before. There was a quiet stillness that didn't seem right.

"Where is everybody?" Sanchez asked one day when there were chores to do. "Where is Slim Pickens? Where are the men? Why doesn't anybody do any work around here?"

"They're all out mending fence," said the cook. "Rock slide took out a section last night."

It was about the same at the B-Bar-X. "Barn needs a new roof," Will Kingman said one day. "Where's Bart? Where are the men?"

"Flash flood at Red Rock," Old Pedro told him. "Quarter of a mile of fence washed out. The men are fixing it."

And so it went for a long time. Rock slides. Floods. Wind. It was always something. Any fence means work, and this was a lot of fence. Sometimes the men were gone for a week at a time, just riding fence, keeping an eye out to see if anything needed fixing.

At last the two ranchers got together and talked things over.

"You know what?" Will Kingman said.

"Yes," said Mario Sanchez, "that fence has got to come down."

"Right!" said Kingman. "Every last mile of it!"

And so they sent the men of the two ranches out to take down the fence. Bart Winslow and the Kingman men rode south. Slim Pickens and the Sanchez men rode north.

When the Sanchez men reached the north end of Razorback Ridge, they set to work digging and prying up fence posts. They rolled up that fence—wire, posts, staples and all. They rolled it along like a wheel. And as they went on digging and prying up posts and rolling and digging and prying and rolling they sang a work song of the West:

> *"Diggin' and rollin'*
> *And diggin' away.*
> *Dig! Dig! Roll!*
> *And roll along!"*

The deep voices echoed through the mountains, and the singing helped the work go better and the fence rolled along, and the roll got bigger.

All along Razorback Ridge the singing echoed. And then in a few days Blue Canyon rang with the rhythm of the singing and the working, and the rolled-up fence got bigger and bigger.

"Say," one of the men said, looking up at the roll, "it's getting mighty high."

"It sure is," said Slim Pickens. "But we've got to keep it rolling. We can't leave it here. It would block the way to Blue Canyon. And besides, it's down hill for the next five miles, so it ought to be easy. Get longer poles. Prop up that roll and keep her steady. She might topple if a wind comes up. Keep her steady and move along, and we'll be home before you know it."

So down the slope the big roll went, and bigger and higher it grew.

"Hold her there!" Slim Pickens suddenly shouted, for one of the prop poles splintered and the big roll leaned at a crazy angle. "Get another pole up there."

"She's toppling!" the men shouted.

"Hold her!"

"Out of the way!"

"Watch out, boys!"

"There she goes!"

And the big roll started down the slope all by
itself, like a giant wheel. Slowly at first, with a
fump fump fump, as the fence posts ripped
from the ground. Then faster it went and the
sound was steady and the fence posts flew and
the roll rolled on.

Down the slope the men ran, shouting and waving their arms. They lashed at the speeding fence with long poles. They hurled their lariats. Finally one lariat caught on a post, then another, and the men held on and slid and tugged and gradually the big roll came to a stop.

"That was a close call," Slim Pickens said. "Keep her steady, boys. We're almost home. I can see the cottonwood trees up ahead."

"Maybe we had better clip this wire here and start a new roll," one of the men suggested. "This one sure is getting big."

"Nothing doing," Slim Pickens said. "We can't leave it here. Too dangerous. If we left it standing here it might start rolling again and no telling where it would stop. And we can't push it over, because if we did it would cover up too much of this good grazing land."

So the men pushed the huge roll to the top of a rise, and they stopped and gave three loud cheers and threw their hats in the air. There, up ahead in Windy Canyon, they could see the buildings of the B-Bar-Bar and the B-Bar-X.

Slim Pickens stood squinting into the distance. There was something else, something beyond the ranch buildings. Something big.

Slim's men went on working and singing. Finally they stopped the roll a hundred yards from the B-Bar-Bar corral.

"Prop her up, boys," Slim said. "Get extra long poles and prop up that roll."

But the men were not listening. They were staring, wide-eyed and open-mouthed. Then Slim saw it and Slim's mouth dropped open, too.

There, coming toward them from the south, was another huge roll of wire. Slim could see the men of the B-Bar-X darting around and propping up the roll with long poles.

Slim's men shuffled out of the way to let the huge roll go by. Bart Winslow and the men of the B-Bar-X worked solemnly, without speaking. One last great push sent the giant wheel against the other wire and a shudder moaned and shook through the two huge rolls.

The men backed away in silent awe. Bart Winslow and Slim Pickens took off their hats. All the men did the same. They leaned back and looked straight up. The second roll was as tall as the first.

That night a high wind blew down the canyon toward the West.

As the men tossed in their bunks they could hear the wind whistling through the big rolls of wire.

By morning the wind had banked a lot of sand against the east side of the wire. Before breakfast was over the wind changed and was blowing up the canyon toward the east. Around noon when the wind died down a lot of sand had banked against the west side of the wire, too.

The men of the two ranches looked at each other and nodded their heads in an understanding way.

Within a few weeks the sand was almost to the top of those rolls of wire. And before long, they were completely covered. Those sandy hills were so high they could be seen for many miles. They became a familiar landmark for pioneers moving westward.

Folks began to call the hills Twin Buttes.

Now, there are a lot of places in the West known as Twin Buttes. But to Will Kingman and Mario Sanchez and all the proud folks around Simpsonville there was only one real Twin Buttes. And that's the one that covers up the biggest fence the West has ever seen.

How Matt Carney Retired and Raised Chickens

O ld Biddy!"

The men in Aunt Marcy's Home-Style Café looked up when they heard the name.

Will Kingman pumped Matt Carney's hand. "Some of Old Biddy's chicks? Here in Simpsonville?"

"That's right," Matt Carney said. "I've been in touch with Old Biddy's owner. And he's selling me three hundred of his prize hens— every single one of them a direct descendant of Old Biddy. Got the signed statement right here in my pocket."

"Who is Old Biddy?" asked a stranger from the East who just happened to be passing through Simpsonville.

The men in the café glanced at each other and smiled.

Jim Beeler laughed right out loud. "Who is Old Biddy?" Beeler said. "Why, Old Biddy was only the rip-snortingest, high-flyingest, out-fightingest and out-egg-layingest hen that ever lived. That's who."

"You bet," Slim Pickens said. "Why, Old Biddy could fly higher than an eagle."

"That's a true fact," Bart Winslow said. "Even the chicken hawks were afraid of Old Biddy."

"And not only that," Sheriff Hardesty said, "one time Old Biddy tackled a hungry coyote and a chicken thief—both at the same time."

"Well, I never heard of anything like that," the stranger from the East said, scratching his head.

"Yep," Bart Winslow said, "Old Biddy lived over in Pinal County. And she was a hen the

West can rightly be proud of. And we're proud to know a man who is going to raise chickens from Old Biddy's brood."

All the men gathered around and slapped Matt on the back.

That was the good thing about Aunt Marcy's café. A man could toss out an idea and discuss it in a perfectly logical and cool-headed manner. This was mighty comforting. It helped a man figure out where he stood on an important matter.

"I think you're nuts," Aunt Marcy said, winging a glob of mashed potatoes onto a platter. "Successful cattle rancher like you? Why don't you let well enough alone? What do you know about raising chickens?"

"Nothing," Matt said truthfully. "But I can learn. I'm tired of wrangling cattle. Always worrying about rustlers! Prices on the cattle market! Trail drives! Hot sun that'd fry the scales off a Gila monster! Rain! Mud!" Matt's voice was rising. He brought his fist down on the table, rattling the knives and forks and the can of milk.

"I'm through with all that," he went on more quietly. "Raising chickens is more civilized. And I'm making myself a little wager. I'm betting that I can do even better in the chicken business than I've done in the cattle business. And if I don't, I'll be the first to admit my mistake—and I'll throw a barbecue and invite everybody in Simpsonville."

Well, the men had another saucer of coffee all around on that.

"I haven't told my wife yet," Matt said. "She sure will be surprised."

"She sure will," Aunt Marcy said. "Who's going to pay for all this grub?"

"Old Biddy!"

Matt Carney's wife turned pale. "Some of Old Biddy's chicks? Here? On our place?"

"That's right," Matt said. "Soon as I sell this next shipment of cattle. I'm quitting the cattle business. I'm going to retire and raise chickens."

That was the good thing about home. A man could toss out an idea and discuss it in a perfectly logical and cool-headed manner. This was mighty comforting. It helped a man figure out where he stood on an important matter.

"Matt Carney, you haven't got the sense you were born with," Mrs. Carney said. "Successful cattle rancher like you? Why don't you let well enough alone? What do you know about raising chickens?"

Then she added, "Anybody who retires to raise chickens has got rocks in his head—Plymouth Rocks." She allowed herself a little chuckle at this.

"Old Biddy wasn't a Plymouth Rock—she was a White Leghorn," Matt said proudly.

"That's even worse," Mrs. Carney said. "All hens are stupid. But White Leghorns have got a slight edge on stupidity over the other breeds."

"Now, Elvira, you don't appreciate real sporting blood," Matt said. "Why, Old Biddy could bring down a chicken hawk in mid-air."

"Vicious!" Mrs. Carney said.

"And one time Old Biddy tackled a hun-

gry coyote," Matt said. "And a famous chicken thief, both at the same time. And the only reason they got away was that Old Biddy was laying an egg at the time and couldn't give them her full attention. Old Biddy sure was game."

"Mean, that's what she was," Mrs. Carney said. "That hen was meaner'n a catamount with a knot tied in its tail."

"Elvira," Matt said, "if I don't do even better in the chicken business than I've done in the cattle business—well, I'll admit my mistake, and I'll throw a barbecue and invite the whole town of Simpsonville."

"You'd better start getting plenty of firewood ready for that barbecue," Mrs. Carney said.

Well, in practically no time Matt wound up his cattle business. He built a fine hen house by the cottonwood tree. He made straw nests. Lots of straw nests. And he put up a shiny wire fence. And the day Matt drove up with the last wagonload of chickens he was as proud as a peacock with an extra set of tail feathers.

Mrs. Carney stood in the kitchen door with her arms folded. "What you got your hand all bandaged up for?" she said.

Matt chuckled. "One of the hens nipped me when I was loading the crates," he said. "Doc took a couple of stitches in it. Nothing serious. These hens sure are game."

"Vicious, that's what they are," Mrs. Carney said.

In the hen yard a big white rooster stretched his neck and started to crow. But before he crowed more than a couple of notes a bunch of the hens flew at him pecking and squawking. The crowing trailed off down the scale to nothing and the rooster ran to a corner of the yard and hid behind a cottonwood stump.

Matt's fine hunting dog, Sir Galahad, stuck his nose through the fence and sniffed at the chickens. A hen flew at him and landed on his nose. Sir Galahad ran yelping to the side of the house.

That was Monday, and that same afternoon a bunch of those hens flew up and attacked a chicken hawk that happened to be flying over. Matt saw a flurry of feathers in the sky and that chicken hawk fell like a rock and bounced off the hen house roof.

"Did you see that?" Matt said. "They're just like Old Biddy. Chips off the old block."

"Vicious, that's what they are," Mrs. Carney said.

The next morning—that was Tuesday—when Matt went out to the chicken yard all three hundred of those hens were lying with their feet in the air and their toes curled. And they were making pathetic little croaking sounds in their throats.

"Stupid chickens!" Mrs. Carney said.

"They just aren't used to their new surroundings," Matt said. "Probably homesick."

So Matt mixed up a big batch of warm chicken mash for them and by afternoon the hens were up and about. "You see?" Matt said. "That's the way with thoroughbreds. High strung."

Mrs. Carney snorted. "Hypochondriacs! That's what they are. They were just pretending to be sick."

On Wednesday morning Matt went out to the hen house to gather the eggs. But there wasn't a hen in sight. Matt ran up and down the rows of nests. Nothing. Not a hen. Not an egg.

Off in the distance he heard cackling. Then more cackling.

He grinned. Of course! Couldn't expect those hens to lay eggs in ordinary straw nests. Not the offspring of Old Biddy. They must have flown over the fence. Yes, sir, they were building their nests somewhere out there on the desert. Under the greasewood bushes, more than likely.

Matt whistled.

His fine hunting dog came running.

"Sir Galahad," Matt said, "go track down those hens. Find those nests. After 'em, boy!" He slapped his knee and pointed toward the greasewood.

Sir Galahad whimpered and backed away.

"What's the matter with you?" Matt said. "I've seen you tackle six mountain lions at once without batting an eye. Are you going to let a few hens bluff you?"

Sir Galahad just stood there whimpering.

Matt turned his back. "Dog," he said, "you're a coward!"

Sir Galahad straightened. With a roar of

defiance he lit out for the greasewood.

There was a flurry of white feathers. Thirty-seven hens flew out of the bushes and landed on Sir Galahad.

And the last Matt saw of that dog he was fording a mirage on the Hassayampa and still going.

Matt stood there kind of stunned.

After a while Matt's wife said, "I think it would be right nice if we were to have a barbecue and invite a lot of folks. I'll just mosey into town and see to the fixings."

And a little later when she drove away in the buggy she called out to Matt, "I'll stay in town with Aunt Marcy tonight. I'll be back tomorrow."

Matt didn't say anything. He just grabbed six of the big hundred-pound sacks of chicken mash. He tore the sacks open with his bare hands and he scattered chicken mash all around the inside of the hen house.

Then Matt got a pair of his wife's big sewing scissors and he sat down to wait. "Old Biddy!" he muttered. "Stupid chickens! I'll show you! We'll see how far you can fly with your wing feathers clipped!"

Before long those hens came flying back over the fence, and started right in eating. They got so busy concentrating on the chicken mash they didn't notice what Matt was doing. Matt grabbed the hens one by one and clipped their long wing feathers.

It took a while to clip those three hundred hens. Matt's hand got tired, but he didn't even slow down. "Stupid chickens!" Matt muttered over and over, keeping time to the click of the scissors.

When Matt was trimming the last hen she squirmed and her beak kind of grazed Matt's hand a little.

"Why, you ornery no-good critters!" Matt yelled. He flung the scissors against the wall. He kicked at the hens and sent them scattering.

Then Matt started in, and he cussed out those hens. First he used the sweet mellifluous language of a bullwhacker caught in the mud. Then he began to warm up and the words flowed even smoother. After that he said some downright personal and insulting things to those hens. And when he was through with that portion of his talk he got down to specific grievances.

"Hypochondriacs!" he yelled, kicking at the hens. He picked up a rock and threw it.

The hens scattered, squawking.

"Sneaky buzzards! Building your nests out in the sticks!"

He threw another rock.

More squawking.

"Chasing off my dog—the finest hunting dog a man ever had!"

Matt picked up another rock. A big one.

But this time he didn't throw it.

Those hens weren't scattering now. They were all moving together, and they were heading straight for Matt.

He dropped the rock.

He backed away.

"Now, girls, I didn't mean—I guess I got a little excited. I . . ."

Matt turned and ran.

He made it to the cottonwood tree just in time.

Well, Matt sat on a high limb looking down at those hens that were descended from Old Biddy. They tried to fly up at Matt, but they couldn't make any headway. Not with their wings clipped that way.

When the sun went down, the big white rooster flew up into the tree and sat on the limb next to Matt.

Well, those hens kept Matt up in that tree all night. And there wasn't anybody for company except the rooster.

That was Wednesday night.

Along toward noon on Thursday, Matt's wife drove up in the buggy. As soon as she saw Matt up in that tree and all those hens down below, Mrs. Carney went in the house and got a broom.

And when the hens saw her coming with the broom, they sauntered off peaceful like and started working on that chicken mash again.

"I got the fixings for a real nice barbecue,

Matt," Mrs. Carney said. "How about Sunday afternoon?"

"That'll be just fine," Matt said.

And he observed that he guessed he would get down out of the tree now, and then he would go into town and invite everybody personally.

It was a great barbecue, and became justly famous all over the West. Folks said the white meat was maybe a mite tough, but the flavor was the finest ever. And all agreed that they had never tasted such gastronomically splendiferous drumsticks—or seen so everlasting many of them.

How Ailments Were Put in Their Proper Place

One of the great things about the West was the way everybody was equal.

This worked out fine as long as there weren't many people to be equal *with*.

But more and more people were moving into the West. And a lot of them landed in Simpsonville. Main Street grew on out past the Wells Fargo office at one end of town, and on out past the livery stable at the other. Tarpaper shanties sprang up right next to fine two-story houses that had stained glass windows and flowers in the yard. Folks said the place was getting so big now they couldn't hear somebody on the other side of town hollering his lungs out.

"With all these new people moving in all the time," Big Jim Beeler said, "it's hard for a man to figure out who he's better than and who he ain't better than. I tell you, our equality is changing something fierce."

"Well, now, Jim, the equality stays the same," Judge Harper explained. "It's the *people* that are getting more different all the time."

One day Sheriff Hardesty announced to his friends that he had a minor ailment. "In fact," the sheriff said, "it's so minor I shouldn't have mentioned it at all. I've got an important job to do, and I'm not going to let a little ailment stop me."

But the sheriff's friends were loyal and helpful and they didn't let things rest there. "Why, sheriff," they said, "your ailment may not be as minor as you think." And they suggested several ways his minor ailment might develop into something more important.

The sheriff listened to these helpful suggestions a while, and he nodded thoughtfully. "Come to think of it," he said, "I believe my ailment *is* getting more important."

The sheriff's friends were proud.

"But I'm not going to let it interfere with duty," the sheriff said. "I'm going right on devoting myself to law and order in Maricopa County—in spite of it all."

The sheriff's friends told it all over town how the sheriff was setting a mighty fine example.

Well, when Mayor Hawkins' friends told him about it, the mayor hit the ceiling. "Boys," he said, "I can't let the sheriff get ahead of me this way. It ain't good politics."

Just about that time, Slick Smith the peddler breezed into town. Among his wares was a fine medical volume that was printed in Parisfrance. The mayor saw his chance to outshine the sheriff, and he bought that medical volume mighty quick.

Well, every word in that volume was written in the French language. And there wasn't a soul in Simpsonville or all Maricopa County who could read or understand one word of French—not even Judge Harper in his fine white house with the iron fence around it.

But the mayor didn't let that stop him. Not a bit of it.

That medical volume was plum full of pictures. Now, those French people are mighty fine artists, and the pictures in that volume were works of art.

The mayor knew when he had found something with tone and class to it, and pretty soon he had gotten himself a fine ailment. And he did it just by studying the pictures in that medical volume. The mayor didn't even know what to call the ailment. But he knew it was imported all the way from Parisfrance, and that made him mighty proud.

The mayor announced it to his friends. And of course before very long a lot of folks were talking about the mayor's imported ailment.

Now, Sheriff Hardesty's friends didn't know

73

just how to break it to the sheriff. Finally they barged in and blurted it right out. "The mayor has got himself a fine ailment, and it's imported all the way from Parisfrance."

The sheriff turned pale.

When he spoke, his voice was hollow. All the spunk and fight seemed to have gone out of him. "Friends," he said, "a man knows when he is beaten, and this is something nobody can fight."

From then on there wasn't any question at all about who was most important in that town. Nobody could outshine the mayor. Nobody. Not even fine folks with clothes from Chicago and rubber-tired buggies drawn by pedigreed thoroughbreds.

The mayor had it all over everybody else. And he didn't let anybody forget it, either.

People saw how handy this was, so they started rating themselves that way, too—by the quality of the ailments they had.

Things were going along fine until Lug Looter almost upset the apple cart. Lug up and announced one day that he had an ail-

ment just as good as the one the mayor had.

Lug Looter! Why, Lug didn't even have regular work. He helped clean the livery stable sometimes, when he wasn't off hunting jack-rabbits or when he didn't just plain sleep all day.

"Do you suppose," Mario Sanchez said, "do you suppose we have to invite Lug to sit at the mayor's table at the Fourth of July picnic?"

"How can we ever figure out who is important and who isn't," Lafe Brimhall whined, "if Lug Looter can come up with an ailment as good as the mayor's?"

Well, it was a mighty confusing situation. Then suddenly things were put back into their right perspective.

A traveling man who said he used to be a horse doctor diagnosed Lug's ailment down to its proper level.

A lot of folks were mighty relieved. But at the same time they were sore at Lug. For a long time nobody would even speak to him, and Lug was downright unhappy and lonely.

Finally one rainy afternoon a group of

kindly disposed citizens gathered on the horse-hair sofas in the lobby of the Elite Hotel. There were Will Kingman and Lafe Brimhall and the ladies of the Maricopa County Benevolent Society. After a short meeting they decided to approach Lug Looter in brotherly charity.

Will and Lafe escorted the ladies over the loose board in front of the hotel. Then they all marched single file down Main Street.

The ladies picked their way through the mud by the stable. They held their heads high and lifted their long skirts daintily as they stepped through the stable doors.

"Lug," said Will Kingman, shaking Lug awake, "we are here to make you a generous offer. We want you to promise that you won't ever again presume to get yourself an ailment that is plum out of your class. If you will promise this, then we will accept you back into the arms of the community as the person you rightfully are—a no-good lazy loafer."

Lug's face beamed. "Oh, I promise," he said. "And I'm mighty grateful to you for your kindness. From now on I won't have any ailment that doesn't befit my low station in the community."

And that's how a lot of folks got to know their position in society.

But there were some folks who just couldn't come up with any ailment at all, no matter how much they put their minds to it.

One day Miss Zeldie Gifford, owner of the Flying B ranch, stormed into Aunt Marcy's Home-Style Café. The screen door slammed loud, and Miss Zeldie marched right up to Bart Winslow's table. "Look here!" she said. "This system is downright unfair. And if anybody can do something about it, you can."

Bart pushed the meat and mashed potatoes over to one side of his mouth. He gulped, stood up politely and removed his hat. "What's the trouble, ma'am?" Bart asked.

"Unfair, that's what it is," she said. "I haven't ever had any kind of ailment in my whole life. But I've got almost as many head of cattle as anybody else. And I've got as many fine dresses as the mayor's wife. Maybe more. And a new brick sidewalk in front of my house—the one in town, that is. Why, I could pay for every bit as good an ailment as anybody in Maricopa County."

Bart scratched his head. "You're right, Miss Zeldie," he said. "You ought to get credit for what you can pay for. And that goes for everybody else, too."

Well, the whole town thought that was a mighty fine idea. And with Bart's help they figured out a system that was fair to everybody. It worked like this: If a person could afford to pay for an ailment, he got credit for it just the same as if he actually had it.

Occasionally some newcomer to town tended to exaggerate an ailment. But you can't fool really smart folks, and those who had heads on their shoulders knew right well who could afford the privilege of what ailments and who couldn't.

So, most folks were content to stick to their own social class and ability to pay. And they were real glad to know just where they fitted into the scheme of things.

All in all, folks considered it a might satis-fying and healthy situation.

How the Sheriff's Posse and the Hold-up Men Sat Down to Dinner Together

The West was becoming more and more civilized—and polite.

For instance, the time the Matson boys relieved the Simpsonville bank of the burden of most of its gold and other worldly possessions.

Luke Matson said, "Thank you," as he held the gun on the bank president and took the bags of gold. And when he ordered Grover and Al to tie up the president and the teller, Luke insisted that his brothers apologize for any inconvenience they had caused the bank.

Sheriff Hardesty had himself a time rounding up a posse. A lot of the men in town already had social engagements. And the sheriff didn't expect a man to break a social engagement just to go tootin' off after a band of outlaws. It wasn't polite.

So the Matsons had a good twenty minute start on him by the time the sheriff got a posse together. There was Bart Winslow and Big Jim Beeler and a bunch of others who didn't have any important social engagements in Simpsonville.

Meanwhile the Matsons had headed straight for the Mexican border.

They rode hard for more than an hour.

All of a sudden Luke Matson pulled up short.

"What are we stopping now for?" Grover asked.

"Yeah," Al said, "let's keep moving. It's still a long way to the border."

But Luke just sat there easy in the saddle. "I surmise," he said, "from the odoriferous aroma coming from that ranch house kitchen over there—I surmise that must be Ma Hadley's place."

" 'Course it is," Grover said. "Everybody knows that's Ma Hadley's place. But we ain't got time to stop now. That sheriff's posse can't be more'n twenty minutes behind us."

"He's right, Luke," Al said, glancing back in the direction of Simpsonville.

"Brothers," Luke said, "I ain't worried about no sheriff's posse. Now, a man in business for hisself, the way we are, well, he has got to observe things and be sensitive to the changing times. And, boys, times *are* changing. The West is becoming civilized—and real polite."

"Maybe so," Grover said, "but I think we ought to high-tail it out of here."

"Brothers," Luke said, "I'm hungry. And I surmise if we was to knock on Ma Hadley's door she wouldn't turn us away without feeding us. I hear tell she's mighty polite."

"That sheriff's posse'll nab us sure," Grover said.

"Brothers," Luke said, "I ain't never had

none of Ma Hadley's cooking. Now, she would be right put out with us if she knew we were this close and didn't drop in for one of her famous meals. Like I said, I'm hungry. I was so took up with business matters back there in Simpsonville, I plum forgot to eat my dinner. Come on, boys."

Well, Grover and Al were still mighty jumpy. But they knew better than to argue with Luke. So the three of them went riding up to the ranch house, looking kind of down on their luck.

Just the sound of hoofbeats made Ma Hadley's face light up. High-born or common folks, it never mattered to Ma as long as there was somebody she could feed. She was that hospitable.

And when she saw these three bedraggled specimens of humanity at her door, she smiled a motherly smile. "Well, hello, strangers," she said. "You do look tired and hungry. Come right in and rest yourselves. What do you know! You're just in time. The turnip greens are almost done, and I'm stirring up a batch of corn dodgers this very minute."

So the Matsons came clomping into Ma Hadley's kitchen. Grover and Al sneaked a look behind the big china cupboard to make certain there wasn't anybody hiding there.

Ma got the boys sat down at the long table. She took her time with the corn dodgers. "Food has got to be prepared just right," she said, "or it isn't fit for a body to eat."

"That's right, ma'am," Luke said. "Why, I hear tell your corn dodgers are so light and fluffy, a man has to eat three at a time so's he'll have something to chew on."

"Pshaw! How folks do talk!" Ma said, smiling.

Grover and Al sat on the edge of their chairs and kept glancing out the window.

Grover whispered to Luke, "Look, Luke, that sheriff's posse will be here any minute. They'll nab us sure."

"Brothers," Luke said, "there's one thing you've got to get through your thick skulls, and that is that things ain't the way they used to be. There is rules today that decent folks

live by."

Ma Hadley set a platter of corn dodgers and a steaming bowl of turnip greens on the table. The Matson boys tied into them and ate like there wasn't any more food in the world.

The boys were hunched over and chewing away when Grover straightened up and cocked an ear. Al twisted around and stared out the window.

A few seconds later the sheriff's posse came thundering into the ranch yard.

Grover and Al jumped out of their chairs

like they were taking off for another climate. Even Luke tensed up a little.

"Why, my lands!" Ma said. "More company! I'll have to set more plates."

Luke eased up and leaned back. "Brothers," he said, "just sit down and relax. Don't you galoots realize we ain't had our dee-sert yet?"

Just about then the sheriff came busting through the door like a ton of dynamite. He took one look at the Matson boys and slapped his gun holster.

"Why, Sheriff Hardesty!" Ma Hadley exclaimed, setting a kettle on the wood range. "How nice to see you! But I've a mind to scold you good for staying away so long. Pull up a chair. I'll have a fresh batch of corn dodgers off the fire in just a spell."

"Well, you see, ma'am," the sheriff said, his hand still on his holster and his eyes on the Matson boys, "we're on kind of urgent business. And besides, we ate just before we found out what happened back in Simpsonville, and so, we..."

"Now, sheriff," Ma Hadley said, "I won't take no for an answer. Nobody goes away from my house without a little something to keep body and soul together. You can't turn down an invitation when it's offered. It isn't polite."

Luke smiled and nodded and went right on chewing.

The posse came in and stood around all tensed up. They watched to see what the sheriff was going to do next.

"I got your places set right over here," Ma Hadley said, indicating the side of the table away from the Matsons.

The sheriff and the posse made a wide circle around the room.

Every eye was on the Matsons.

The sheriff sidled into a chair across the table from Luke.

Ma Hadley set a big platter of corn dodgers and a bowl of steaming turnip greens in front of the sheriff.

Before long the sheriff and the posse were hunched over and wading into those corn dodgers and turnip greens.

The Matson boys got through eating first, of course, because they started first.

Luke pushed his chair back from the table.

The sheriff stopped chewing. His eyes were glued on Luke.

Grover and Al slunk toward the door.

"Brothers!" Luke called sharply.

Grover and Al stopped in their tracks.

"Brothers! Don't you know it ain't polite to eat and run like that? Now, you come on back here."

Grover and Al slunk back and slid into their chairs.

89

"That's better," Luke said. He drew his sleeve across his mouth kind of slow and polite. He leaned back easy and comfortable and hooked his thumbs in his belt. He exchanged a few casual remarks with Ma Hadley about the weather. Then he said, "Things are getting mighty nice and civilized. The West has come to be a right pleasant location to live in."

"That's the honest truth," Ma Hadley said over her shoulder. She hummed a little tune as she moved pots and pans around on the stove.

Luke stood up.

The sheriff slapped his gun holster.

The posse raised up out of their chairs.

"Why, my goodness, sheriff," Ma Hadley said, opening the oven. "I almost forgot about this batch of apple pies. Oh, pshaw! They're a mite over-done."

"Ma Hadley, ma'am," Luke said, "that was mighty good eating. You're a real comfort to a hungry man. We thank you kindly for your hospitality, don't we, brothers?"

Grover and Al muttered their thanks and

headed for the door.

"It's nice to have company," Ma said as she pulled a pie from the oven.

Luke moved toward the door. Slow. Like there wasn't any hurry in the world.

The sheriff's hand tightened on his gun butt.

Luke stopped.

Ma Hadley was peering into the big coffee pot on the back of the stove. "Sheriff," she said, "how about another cup of coffee for you and your men? To go with your pie."

The sheriff moved his hand away from his gun.

The posse settled back in their chairs.

Luke let out his breath and moseyed on. At the door he paused, smiling. He made a polite bow to Ma Hadley to show he knew he was in civilized society. "Thank ya again, ma'am," he said. "Thank ya kindly."

"Y'all come back again, now, y'hear?" Ma said.

The door closed.

A few seconds later the sheriff heard the

Matson boys gallop off for the border with all that loot from the Simpsonville bank.

The sheriff and posse had another cup of coffee all around, and a sizeable slab of Ma Hadley's hot apple pie.

Finally the sheriff pushed his chair back from the table. "By the way, ma'am," he said, "did you know that Judge Harper's daughter is going to a fine finishing-up school back East?"

"Well, now, that's nice," Ma Hadley said. "Such a sweet girl, too."

"Most of the wells in the area are maintaining their water level pretty fair," the sheriff observed.

"Isn't that wonderful!" Ma Hadley said. "And the spring seepage ought to bring the level up even higher."

The sheriff trimmed a couple of fingernails, and then he said, casual like, "We certainly do thank you for the fine meal, ma'am. Your cooking is justly famous all over the West."

"It sure is, ma'am," said Bart Winslow, smiling very mannerly.

"Best grub I ever eat," Big Jim Beeler said.

Ma Hadley fluttered a little, but you could see she was real pleased. "Oh, pshaw! It was nothing," she said.

The posse all nodded politely to Ma Hadley. They wandered out one by one. They moseyed along like they didn't have any place to go in particular, but their eyes darted toward their horses.

The sheriff followed them out and walked slow to the hitching rack.

He untied his horse.

"So nice to see you folks again," Ma Hadley said.

"Thank you kindly, ma'am," the sheriff said, and eased into the saddle.

The sheriff roweled his horse's flank.

The horse wheeled.

Hooves struck sparks.

"Y'all come back, y' hear?" Ma Hadley called.

The sheriff lifted his hat and smiled.

The dust swallowed the sheriff and posse.

"After them, men!" the sheriff roared above

the hoofbeats. "We've got to catch them before they get to the border!"

Well, that's just a sample of how civilized and polite the West was getting to be. Why, not long after that, the stage to Tombstone was heading through Apache Pass one day when all of a sudden the—but that's another story and another book, and this is the end of this one.